W9-CNA-250

Mary had a Little Lamb

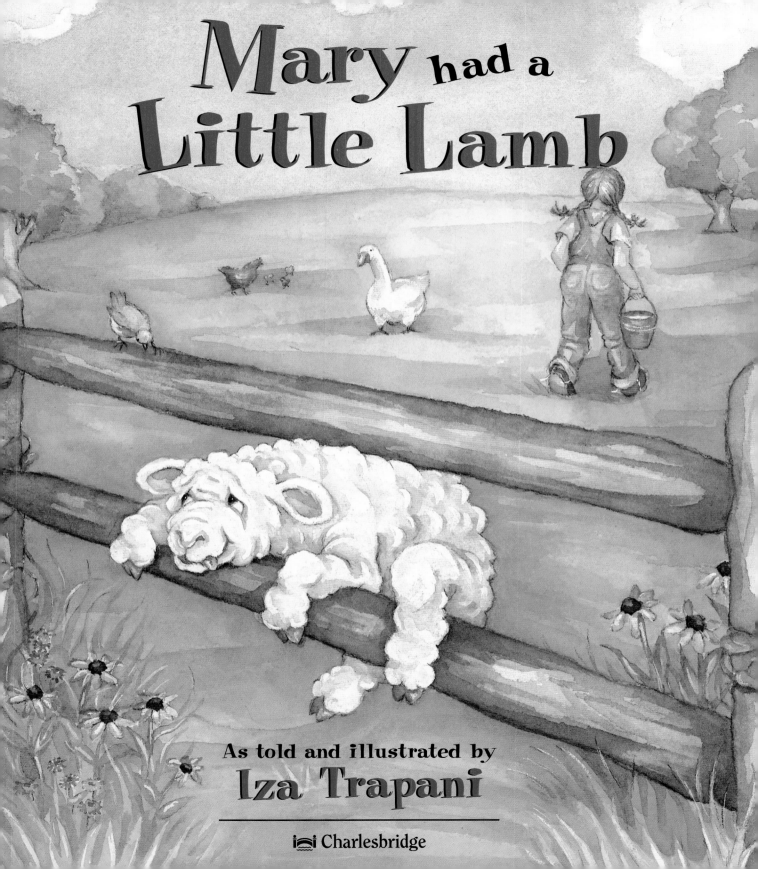

Mary had a Little Lamb

As told and illustrated by
Iza Trapani

Charlesbridge

First paperback edition 2003
Copyright © 1998 by Iza Trapani

Published by Charlesbridge
85 Main Street
Watertown, MA 02472
(617) 926-0329
www.charlesbridge.com

Library of Congress Cataloging-in-Publication Data
Trapani, Iza.
Mary had a little lamb / as told and illustrated by Iza Trapani.
1 v. (unpaged) : col. ill. ; 25 cm.
Summary: This expanded version of the traditional rhyme shows what happens
when the lamb decides to go off alone. Includes music on the last page.
ISBN 978-1-58089-009-0 (reinforced for library use)
ISBN 978-1-58089-090-8 (softcover)
ISBN 978-1-60734-554-1 (ebook)
ISBN 978-1-60734-097-3 (ebook pdf)
1. Children's songs. [1. Children's songs—Texts.
2. Sheep—Songs and music. 3. Songs.] I. Title.
PZ8.3.T686   Mak 1998
782.42164'0268—dc21   98-014728

Printed in China
(hc) 10 9 8 7 6 5 4 3 2
(sc) 10

Text set in 16-point Tiffany Medium
Printed by Imago in China
Book production and design by *The Kids at Our House*

For Rob and Gabe,
I love ewe with all my heart!

Mary had a little lamb.
Its fleece was white as snow,
And everywhere that Mary went
The lamb was sure to go.

And then one day the little lamb
Decided to be free,
And so it wandered off alone
To see what it could see.

Across the field, up to the barn
The little lamb did stray,
And there it met a big brown horse
And let it out to play.

But when the gate was opened up
The horse went charging out,
And in its dust the little lamb
Went stumbling all about.

It bumped into the tough old goose
As she was walking by.
She flapped her wings and hissed and pecked,
Which made the poor lamb cry.

The cow woke up and kicked a pail
Right up into the air,
And gave the lamb a milky bath
As it was standing there.

The little lamb raced back outside
Escaping, taking off,
But as it ran it tripped and fell
Into the water trough.

The lamb stood up and shook its fleece
But did not realize
The old barn cat would surely get
A very wet surprise.

The cat let out a shriek so loud,
It gave the hens a scare
And made them cluck and run around
In circles everywhere.

In the middle of this fuss,
A grumpy goat came by
And gave the lamb a mean old butt
Straight up into the sky.

Into the pigpen fell the lamb
And got completely stuck,
Then all the way from head to hoof
Was covered up in muck.

When Mary found her little lamb,
Its fleece was muddy brown.
She cleaned it up with lamb shampoo
And gently hosed it down.

She brushed and fed the little lamb
And kissed its sleepy head.
It looked at her with sheepish eyes
And then it went to bed.

Mary had a Little Lamb

Ma - ry had a lit - tle lamb, it's fleece was white as snow and

eve - ry - where that Ma - ry went the lamb was sure to go.

2. And then one day the little lamb
   Decided to be free,
   And so it wandered off alone
   To see what it could see.

3. Across the field, up to the barn
   The little lamb did stray,
   And there it met a big brown horse
   And let it out to play.

4. But when the gate was opened up
   The horse went charging out,
   And in its dust the little lamb
   Went stumbling all about.

5. It bumped into the tough old goose
   As she was walking by.
   She flapped her wings and hissed and pecked,
   Which made the poor lamb cry.

6. The cow woke up and kicked a pail
   Right up into the air,
   And gave the lamb a milky bath
   As it was standing there.

7. The little lamb raced back outside
   Escaping, taking off,
   But as it ran it tripped and fell
   Into the water trough.

8. The lamb stood up and shook its fleece
   But did not realize
   The old barn cat would surely get
   A very wet surprise.

9. The cat let out a shriek so loud,
   It gave the hens a scare
   And made them cluck and run around
   In circles everywhere.

10. In the middle of this fuss,
    A grumpy goat came by
    And gave the lamb a mean old butt
    Straight up into the sky.

11. Into the pigpen fell the lamb
    And got completely stuck,
    Then all the way from head to hoof
    Was covered up in muck.

12. When Mary found her little lamb,
    Its fleece was muddy brown.
    She cleaned it up with lamb shampoo
    And gently hosed it down.

13. She brushed and fed the little lamb
    And kissed its sleepy head.
    It looked at her with sheepish eyes
    And then it went to bed.